for Mum and Dad

MYRIAD BOOKS LIMITED
35 Bishopsthorpe Road, London SE26 4PA

First published in 1999 by
PICCADILLY PRESS LIMITED
5 Castle Road, London NW1 8PR
www.piccadillypress.co.uk

ISBN 1 904736 70 X

Designed by Louise Millar
Cover designed by Judith Robertson

Printed in China

Toffee
in trouble

Sally Chambers

MYRIAD BOOKS LIMITED

Tweet! Tweet! Tweet!
The birds are waking up.
Toffee wakes up too
and stretches.

It's very quiet.

Everyone's asleep.

But Toffee wants to play!

What's that noise in the bathroom?

Drip Drip Drip

It's just the tap.

What's that noise in the playroom?

Maybe someone else is awake.

Buzz Buzz Buzz

It's only a fly!

Toffee chases the fly . . .

through the door,

and down the stairs.   But the fly buzzes off.

Then Toffee sees the newspaper.

Rustle!

Rustle!

Rustle!

Toffee always loves playing
with the newspaper.

Tweet! Tweet! Tweet!
The birds are singing louder now.

Perhaps they will play with Toffee.

But all the birds fly away!

Crash! Bang!
Smash! Here comes Toffee, back again!

Now everyone is awake.
Oh dear! What an awful mess!

Where is that cat?
Toffee, you're in such trouble!

Oh . . . Toffee!